CURE FOR THE SLEEPING WOMAN

T. M. Adair

ISBN: 1-949219-00-3
ISBN-13: 978-949219-00-5

DEDICATION

Thanks, Dean, for urging me to write the next sentence
and finish the story.

CURE FOR THE
SLEEPING WOMAN

The line to enter the exhibit of the Sleeping Woman at the Clarkston Historical Museum went out the door and around the corner. Which, to be fair, was not that far a distance since the museum's entry was just a mud room in a restored New England saltbox, and the door from the mudroom to the outdoors was only a few steps from the street corner. Still, Effie Gennings had never before seen so many people waiting in her line. She stood at the little podium in the renovated-but-not-authentic, Arts & Crafts-style entry way and smiled politely. Where had all these townsfolk been when she had presented the Clarkston Rail Days exhibit? Or the Founder's Finds revolving display, after months of research?

Now people were just here so they could say they'd seen the Sleeping Woman, found mummified in the Anderson's peat bog when a town crew was excavating in order to install a drainage pipe across the bog. The crew that found the body called her The Sleeping Woman, and the name had stuck. The Sleeping Woman was on display now, until the good folks from the University were able to come take her away, and Effie sure wished they would hurry.

Technically, though, the Sleeping Woman wasn't supposed to be on display, and therefore Effie was probably not supposed to be collecting ticket money. The Museum was the temporary repository of the remains of the poor woman only because the Museum had the right size climate-controlled display case to hold the body until experts could arrive. Who knew how long the poor thing had been in that bog? Effie wasn't an expert on mummification, but she had a history degree. And both history and common sense told her that anyone found in the local peat bog ended up there by foul play.

The mummy was an eerie reminder that what went into the earth couldn't remain unchanged. This region's original Mohawk inhabitants had stayed far away from the bog, calling the waters, the scrubby brush and reeds, and even the air of the bog evil. Later European settlers had avoided it as well, following the Mohawk example.

Effie knew all of the people in her line by face and most of them by name. There was Jim, from the town Water Department, who had cajoled Dougie and the others from the Highway Department into helping move the old Salton Homestead onto the Historical Society grounds when Portia Salton had passed away. All of Portia's quilt collection had been bequeathed to the Museum, including some well-preserved Colonial examples. For now, they'd been moved to outside storage in order to make room for the Sleeping Woman in the museum proper.

Behind Jim was a group of younger women. Effie recognized their faces from the summer craft show. One was a potter, and Effie had bought one of the potter's hand-thrown lotion dispensers. It was glazed in a combination of russet and blue, and the seam between the body and the pump dispenser leaked a bit if you angled it wrong. But that was to be expected with a one of a kind, hand-made item. Little flaws made it more unique.

Effie didn't know how many more people waited outside, but she would find out soon enough. Meanwhile, she kept a sharp eye on Eddie Adams, who waited at the front of her line. Eddie ran the gas station just across the corner. He stood at her podium running the index finger of his right hand back and forth on the wooden edge. An index finger which she hoped was not as greasy as the stains on the back of his hand might indicate.

The Eddie in front of her was born Eddie Adams III, and his son was Eddie Adams IV. Not Edward, Eddie. Eddie II was a nice guy who got along with everyone, and Eddie III was all right, if a little oblivious of personal space sometimes, like now. But Eddie IV was a drug-dealing dropout from the local community college and she hoped for Eddie II and Eddie III's sake that Eddie IV would get his act together before he killed himself or someone else.

"Who's minding the shop?" Effie finally asked, tugging discreetly on the jacket of her best navy pantsuit to straighten it. She wished Eddie would stop touching her podium. And hoped he wouldn't smudge anything in the Museum, especially the whitewashed walls which were a bear to clean.

"Eddie's there," he said.

Effie smiled more broadly. Pretend you didn't hear that, she told herself. Be polite.

"I mean, Dad's there," Eddie corrected himself. He lifted his right hand and ran it through his hair. Effie was relieved to see that his palms and fingers seemed clean. He was wearing his garage work pants and a flannel shirt, and they looked clean, too. He must have changed out of his work clothes before coming over.

"I saw your dad this morning," she said. "He was first in line when I opened up."

"Yep."

Eddie II had been waiting for her to unlock the place, bundled up in his usual red buffalo check barn coat, though Effie had thought the morning just crisp, not cold.

"I'm sure your turn will be soon."

Eddie III nodded.

Effie returned her face to a practiced, polite smile and nodded back.

There wasn't enough space in the textile room for more than a handful of visitors, not with the glass case, currently occupied by the Sleeping Woman, taking up so much space in the center of the room. Well, not at any time, really. Effie and the co-manager of the Museum, Deena, were letting people in one at a time, to avoid a crush or any damage to the case or it's electronics. Effie waited out here and took ticket money. Deena monitored activity inside, because you couldn't trust people, not even people you knew for years. Maybe especially those you'd known for years. You never knew what was going on inside someone's head. Probably someone would get the idea to take home a little souvenir, break off a piece of the Sleeping Woman. Which was just creepy.

"We'll let you in as soon as the person in there is through viewing."

"Yep."

Apparently, there wasn't going to be much conversation. Eddie glanced at the ladies at the back of the line. Jim had turned around to talk to them.

"It will be five dollars," Effie said.

Eddie nodded and with a flick of his wrist made a five appear in his hand.

She'd forgotten about Eddie's cute sleight-of-hand tricks. They had graduated together at Clarkston High, and he'd done magic tricks of one sort or another in every one of the annual talent shows. Card tricks, making a rabbit appear or disappear into a hat, that sort of thing.

Effie took the five and put it into the green metal cash box behind the podium. It had been her brother's first tackle box when they were kids, so it was banged up and rusted, but did the job fine as a cash box. Especially since this place hardly ever saw any cash. If it weren't for legacy gifts made as one or another of the local residents passed away, the Museum would have trouble even paying the light bill.

Eddie began running his finger across the podium edge again.

She wasn't going to ask if she would have the pleasure of Eddie IV's presence later today. If Eddie didn't want to make any conversation, she'd just wait in silence for Deena to step out to say that he could go in to view the Sleeping Woman.

*

Effie squeezed past Deena Wavens, who stood holding the door to the display room open, and slipped into the dimly lit space. Deena was heavy-set without seeming to be too heavy, due to her almost six-foot height. Effie kept herself trim and slim, but then she didn't have Deena's five children and three grandchildren. Effie didn't have any children at all. She had her history degree, and the classes she taught at Clarkston Community

College, and her yoga classes—also at the College—and her little cottage just outside of town, perfectly sized for one. And, of course, she had the Museum.

"How long do you need?" Effie whispered.

"Just give me a while out here so I can rest my feet, and I'll be good to go again," Deena whispered back. Effie was surprised to see Deena's four-inch spike-heeled pumps held in one hand. But then, she had to look up to Deena regardless whether the woman wore heels or not.

"We should shut down for dinner," Effie said. "You'll need more than a few minutes hiding in your stocking feet behind the podium to recover from wearing those all afternoon."

"Let's see how the crowds go," Deena said. "The University folks could get here tonight. I want to get as many people through here as possible before they show up and shut us down. We need the ticket money."

Effie turned toward the glass display case and waited for her eyes to adjust to the thin light. "Take your time," she said. "I'm wearing flats."

It was long past being her turn, anyway. She'd left Deena all alone in here with the Sleeping Woman and the slow parade of townsfolk, part of the morning and all afternoon, because Effie found the whole situation creepy and a little distasteful.

It wasn't any better now. The only light in the room came from the baseboard and crown molding lights around the perimeter. Built-in glass-front cabinets lined two walls, and pine cabinets lined the other two. The cabinet shelves were empty now. Effie cringed at the thought of all the Depression Glass wrapped in newspaper and stacked in the trunk of her Honda. It would be filthy when they brought it back out, but at least all that could be cleaned with soap and water.

Deena let Eddie III past her and shut the door behind him with a soft click.

"I thought there were other people in here," Eddie said. "No one came out."

Effie angled her head toward the door opposite them. "That leads to the back storage, and from there, out to the back porch. We're trying to bring people in one door and out the other."

Eddie stepped up next to her and looked at the display case.

"Doesn't look like she's sleeping," Eddie said.

"Mmm-hmm." Effie stepped forward and looked down at the small readout near the foot-end of the display case. Until the Sleeping Woman arrived, it had been the east end of the case, not the foot-end. The temperature and humidity were right where she had set them, following directions from the University. Considering that the University was just a hop, skip and a jump away, she didn't understand why they hadn't sent someone over yet. She and Deena were into their fourth day since the Clarkston Museum had been made temporary custodian of the Sleeping Woman, and their third with the body on display.

"Is that a blanket she's wrapped in? It looks like plastic. Or maybe leather," Eddie said.

Eddie had been quiet in line, but now he wanted to chat? Effie steeled herself before answering. She should have asked Deena to stay in here, stocking feet or no.

"The Sleeping Woman is wrapped in a fabric of some kind which has been changed by the natural action of the chemicals in the peat bog over the years," she said.

Once she got started, her practiced patter came more easily. "It is wrapped around her like a swaddling cloth, so that only her face is visible. Her body lays nearly straight inside the cloth, unlike prehistoric mummies found in peat bogs in Europe. There is no visual evidence of damage to the Sleeping Woman's body so we cannot tell how she died until the University examines her."

Eddie frowned, ruffling his graying black hair while he thought about what she said. "How do you know all that?"

"Google," she shrugged. "Plus what the Professor told me after he got the email with the pictures."

"But her face is almost the same as the blanket," Eddie said. "How can that be?"

Effie shrugged again. It bothered her to see the skin stretched across the Sleeping Woman's face so tightly. As if it had shrunk down onto her bones. The same way that Effie's vacuum sealer pulled thick plastic tight against whatever leftover chicken or veggies she wanted to freeze. As if the woman had been no more in life than some leftover.

"The peat bog does that to skin, too, it seems."

"Is that hair? What color do you think it is?"

Honestly, she wished Eddie would shut up. He was leaning over the display case, his face above the Sleeping Woman's, as if he were the Prince Charming to her Sleeping Beauty.

"I think it's hair, anyway." Eddie leaned closer. "Maybe she's blond?"

"Don't touch the glass, Eddie," Effie said, suddenly worried. "Don't lean on the glass, don't touch the glass, don't—"

Too late. Eddie had one hand on the top of the case and he pushed off when he registered her words.

Effie pulled him back away from the case by one arm.

Now there were fingerprints on the glass. Now she was going to have to clean it, and right up there by the Sleeping Woman's face, too. Why did they call her a Sleeping Woman, anyway? She didn't look more than fifteen years old, to Effie. Not that she knew what a fifteen year old mummified bog girl looked like. But she seemed too small to be full grown, and her face was so thin, and the fabric shrunken around her made her arms—crossed across her chest with her hands clenched in two fists—and her legs—straight and pressed close together at the ankles—stand out in high relief. And she didn't look like she was sleeping, not the way morticians tried to make a corpse seem at a viewing. As if people thought death and sleep were the same thing.

"Gees, Effie, I'm sorry," Eddie said. "I didn't mean to upset you."

Effie still clung to his arm as if he was

going to pull away from her, but he didn't. So embarrassing. Had she squeaked when he touched the case? As if he was breaking it? It was just a few fingerprints, right? And she was a historian for goodness sake. What was a few fingerprints in the scale of history?

The room closed in around her, and she gripped Eddie's arm tighter, just above the elbow, trying to keep herself from swaying and all the time thinking she should let go, but she couldn't, or perhaps it was just that her hand wouldn't obey her. The air in the room seemed hotter, and Eddie's fingerprints on the glass grew larger until they were all she could really see, she couldn't even see the Sleeping Women for the fingerprints, and then she couldn't see anything clearly at all because her eyes couldn't focus through all the water.

She was crying, and she knew she didn't want to cry, but there it was. She was still crying even though she wanted to stop her tears. The Sleeping Woman was here, suddenly of interest, suddenly putting Clarkston Historical Museum on the map, and Eddie could have ruined it all. Or maybe she was ruining it all, right now.

It wasn't fair, and that's what hurt the worst. Nothing Effie had ever done to show the town the importance of its own history had ever mattered a lick compared to this one Sleeping Woman they knew nothing about. And even if she had known something about this poor girl, the townspeople would only care for the notoriety, how the Sleeping Woman put the Anderson's bog on the map for something besides boggy-ness. The Sleeping Woman herself meant nothing to them.

Effie wished she knew some of the Mohawk people. The woman was probably one of their ancestors, right? Goodness, if the Mohawk elders knew the Museum was showing their mummy, they'd probably shut the place down with protests. What had she and Deena been thinking?

Let them take it—her—back to Mohawk ground, let them display her if they wanted to, until the University got around to showing up. People could come visit the Sleeping Woman and then have dinner at the Mohawk casino. The Nation could even take the display case with them. No way would she ever be able to look at it again without seeing a dead girl eerily wrapped in filthy rags, remembered for nothing, her face muddied and masked for eternity.

And how was she supposed to clean the case? What kind of chemicals removed whatever residue a dead body left behind? Not to mention the damage from the acidity of the peat bog itself. The Mohawk Nation could have the case and all the expensive electronics that went with it. She'd find another solution for displaying Portia's quilts and the old letters and maps that had been in the case a few days ago.

Anything, just to get this awful mummy out of her museum and away from the displays that, she hated to admit, probably no one was going to bother to come visit once the Sleeping Woman was gone.

And she was still crying, and thinking about how to get hand prints off the case without having to get too close to the body. Imagine that, a history major, and here she was blubbering over having to get close to a dead body. Good thing she hadn't taken up archeology. Of course, she couldn't have traveled or gone on digs, couldn't have left Clarkston after her mom turned ill. Goodness, is that what her mother would look like if you dug her body up?

*

"Yeah, I think she's done for the day. Better tell them to come back in the morning." Eddie had cracked the door to the foyer-turned-mud room and was whispering to Deena.

Effie was sitting on the floor, her knees pulled up to her chest, hugging herself, and still sniffling. And crushing the crepe of her best pantsuit.

Eddie sat down on the floor to her right and leaned back against the pine cabinet doors. He pulled his knees up and rested his hands across them.

"I guess this whole thing bothers you," he said.

Effie rolled her eyes and wiped her nose with the back of her left hand. "You think?"

"Yeah, kinda," Eddie deadpanned, looking straight ahead at the foot-end of the case.

"What gave me away?" she asked. "The crying? The sniffling?" She was trying to make a joke but it wasn't working.

"Nah, it was you putting your fingernails through my elbow," Eddie finally looked at her. He held up his elbow. "I think I might need stitches."

"Ha, ha. There's not even a scratch in your flannel."

Eddie grinned. "Made you laugh." He pulled a deck of cards out from a back pocket and fanned them out in front of her. "Pick a card?"

"Are you serious? It's disrespectful."

"Well I'm not asking you to throw a party in here or something," he said. "Just take a card."

Effie pulled a card from the middle of the deck.

"Now look at the card, but don't show me," Eddie said, "then put it back in the deck, anywhere you like."

"Fine. Don't look," Effie said.

Eddie turned his head away from her.

She looked at her card: the three of diamonds. Eddie still held the deck in his left hand, waiting for her to replace the card. "I want to shuffle," she said.

"Go ahead," he handed her the deck.

She slid her card into the deck and shuffled it twice before giving the cards back to him.

"Good bridge," he said. He took the cards and dealt them into three even piles on the sage green carpet, face up. "Pay attention to which pile your card is in, but don't tell me the card," he said as he dealt.

"Now point out which pile your card is in."

Effie pointed. Eddie re-stacked the cards and repeated the procedure, again asking her to tell him which pile her card was in. Then he did it a third time. He may have complimented her shuffling, but she could see he was confident with his hands. The cards slipped through them softly, almost as if he was playing a musical instrument.

Finally, he began flipping cards face up, until he reached the three of diamonds.

"That your card?" he asked.

"How'd you do that?"

"Fate was in the air," he said, mimicking a mysterious stage voice.

"Very funny."

"Well, you know I can't tell you the secret. Magician's honor and all that."

Effie sighed. He'd distracted her long enough. "Why were you looking so close at her?" she asked. "Are you really that interested?"

Eddie flushed and looked away. "I guess I just had to be sure," he said.

"Sure of what?"

"I know it sounds crazy," he said. He pocketed his cards and stood, then reached a hand down to Effie. She took it, and he pulled her to her feet. "I just had to be sure if it was Patricia or not."

"Oh," Effie nodded. "You thought it might have been?" Patricia was Patricia Evans, Eddie IV's mother, and she'd disappeared soon after the boy was born. No one really asked Eddie III about her. He'd been so obviously heartbroken about her leaving that at first no one dared. And then as time passed, it was too awkward to ask, she supposed. At least, too awkward for her.

"Dad said it wasn't her," he said, looking down at his feet. "First, he said it couldn't be. Then he came here and looked, and confirmed it wasn't her. I didn't want to come here myself. I didn't really think he could be wrong. But then, I had to see for myself."

Patricia had been a couple years behind them in school. Effie didn't know her well but she knew enough to know this girl wasn't Patricia. Nor anyone else Effie had ever known. If the University Professor was right, this girl lived maybe a few hundred years ago. She didn't know if the Professor could tell that by looking at pictures or if he was just hoping.

"It isn't Patricia," she said softly.

Eddie smiled sadly. "No, it's not. I guess that's good. I wouldn't like to think that Patricia was alone in that water all these years."

*

It wasn't quite sunset yet when Effie locked

the deadbolt on the front door of the Clarkston Historical Museum. Eddie stood below her, on the sidewalk, waiting. He'd sent Deena home a while back, and then waited while Effie washed her face and tried to make herself look presentable in the tiny powder room off the mud room. Then she had to lock the back door, close up the back room. She'd decided to leave cleaning Eddie's prints off the glass until tomorrow.

"You can head out," Effie said. "I'm fine."

She didn't feel fine. What she felt was embarrassed. New kid in school, tripped and spilled your lunch on the cool guy embarrassed. She turned her back to the locked door and looked up at the sky. Another crisp night. The air was still. Even though she'd scrubbed hard, she knew there were still stubborn smudges of mascara under her eyes.

"I'll walk you to your car," Eddie said.

That was nice of him, but she didn't want him thinking she couldn't take care of herself. Because she could. Take care of herself. Just because the situation had gotten to her a bit didn't mean she couldn't walk to her car—parked right around back—and drive herself home.

"I'm fine, really," she said, coming down

the steps to stand beside him. "Eddie must wonder where you've been all this time."

Across the street at the corner, the lights were on inside the garage. The two lift doors were pulled shut, but the gas pumps were lit and the Open sign on the convenience store side of the garage blinked brightly in tall, neon-white letters.

"I called him while you were freshening up," Eddie said. "Dad's minding the shop. It's his night anyway. His friends will be over soon to play cards while they hang out with him."

"Shoot," Effie said, looking back at the Museum. A bit of light leaked out at the bottom of one of the windows. "I left a light on."

Eddie shrugged. "Don't you usually leave some on?"

"The ones on timers, yes. They're programmed so I don't have to remember to set them every day. But not that one. That's inside the display room." Effie sighed. She really didn't want to go back in there. She really didn't want to go back in there alone, and she really didn't want to ask Eddie to go with her. She didn't want to be as needy as she felt. This whole situation unnerved and irritated her.

"I don't remember there being a window in there," Eddie said.

"It's behind one of the cabinets," Effie said. "Light isn't good for our artifacts, so we put one of the cabinets in front of the window, but it isn't boarded over or anything."

"Okay." Eddie stepped up to the door and unlocked it. "I'll get it," he said.

"Hey, wait! How'd you—"

Eddie grinned over his shoulder at her. He held up her keys and jingled them. "Magician, remember?"

"Thief, more like," she grumbled, but she was laughing a bit, too, as she hurried after him. She'd had the keys in her hand, and hadn't felt him take them from her. When had he done it? As touchy as she felt right now, how had she not noticed?

The mud room was dark, so light shone brightly under the crack of the door to the display room. Effie stepped into the dark, pulling the front door shut behind her.

"I think you'd better come see this," Eddie said. His voice came from inside the display room now.

"What?" Effie felt her blood pressure rising. This job, once so enjoyable, was going to kill her. They had only stepped out a minute ago. What could have gone wrong?

She stood in the display room doorway and a sudden movement startled her.

"Boo!"

Someone rushed toward her and without hesitation she stomped down hard. She caught the edge of a foot, and shoved with all her might at the bulk of the form. No thinking, just reacting, like they taught in self-defense class.

A heavy thump sounded, with a near-simultaneous "oomph."

"That didn't go the way I expected," Eddie said. His voice came from somewhere near the level of her knees.

"Are you trying to scare me? Eddie Adams the Third! What in the world were you thinking?" Effie felt around the doorway for the main light switch while she talked. The Sleeping Woman had endured a thousand years in the bog. Surely, she could survive a few moments of incandescent light.

Effie flipped the light switch on. Eddie sat on the floor, blinking up at her. He squinted, and rubbed a hand over his face before talking.

"I was just trying to lighten the mood," he said.

"By scaring me to death? How does that lighten the mood?"

"Gees, Effie, I'm sorry," he said. "I guess that sort of thing works better in our house, with just us guys," He reached up to her and she grabbed his hand, helping him up.

Standing now, he was a little too close for her comfort. He had big gray eyes in this light. In sunlight, she thought, his eyes were probably the palest blue. His dark hair was threaded with gray and cut short. It stood up a little now where he had pushed at it, and she resisted the urge to smooth it out. The light in the room even caused a bit of reflection off his bit of five o'clock beard.

"I can't believe you did that," she said. She felt a little like she was reprimanding a child. Or as if maybe she was making too big a deal of the situation. How was she supposed to act?

Eddie had the grace to look a bit ashamed. "I can't believe you used my whole name to yell at me," he said.

"Well, I didn't use your middle name."

Eddie flushed deep red. "Let's hope things don't get bad enough you have to do that," he said.

Effie giggled. She was appalled at herself for giggling and covered her mouth, as if she could stop the giggle from coming out, but another came out anyway.

"Don't say it," Eddie warned, but he was laughing a bit now, too.

Effie finally gave up and leaned against the door frame, laughing outright. "It's like your Kryptonite, that name, is it?" she asked. "I guess I have a secret weapon to use on you now."

"You wouldn't dare," he said.

Well, she probably wouldn't, but he didn't need to know that. She wasn't too fond of her own middle name, Eustace, and probably Eddie didn't much like having the middle name Stetson. She pretended to think about it, one hand on her chin and head tilted to the side. "Considering you almost scared me to death, I don't know…"

"Aww, come on, Effie, be a good sport."

She snorted. "I'm always a good sport," she said. "Maybe too good a sport."

Eddie cocked his head at her and opened his mouth to say something, but then the phone rang. Not her cell phone, nor his, but the phone sitting on the side table in the mud room, the land line for the Museum.

*

Effie and Eddie sat in the little mud room on the long bench under the one window, lights blazing in the Museum. Sunset was over now, not that you could see it from here since the other buildings on the street blocked the western view. In a bigger house, this would have been a window seat. In this little salt box, it was a built-in that ran the length of one short wall. Effie sat with her back to the long wall and her stocking feet up on the seat. Eddie sat perpendicular to her, leaning against the short wall.

"Won't be too long now," she said. She knew she should be happy, or at least accepting, but she was neither. When the Sleeping Woman was gone, Effie's life would return to normal. Maybe that was the problem. Maybe normal was the problem.

"Can't believe they're sending someone so late," Eddie said.

"I can't believe they didn't send someone right away," she said.

"That, too," he agreed.

"And then what?"

"What do you mean?"

"Until now, no one bothered to even look at this place," Effie said. "What happens when the Sleeping Woman is gone? Do we go back to being invisible?"

Eddie nodded as if he was a sage from the farthest mountaintop. "Whatever you do, it will be fine," he said.

"You can't know that."

"It's how things go," he said.

Effie tried to look him in the eyes, but he was looking down at his feet. There was a sadness in him that seemed almost bottomless, she thought.

"I don't know if it is how things go," she said softly. "Maybe they ought to go differently."

Eddie shrugged. "There's always lots of options," he said. "Problem is, there aren't that many end results."

"All roads lead to Rome?"

"Something like that," Eddie said. "Good Rome, or Bad Rome. Still, they lead to Rome."

Effie was worried she had depressed him. Goodness, she was a lousy friend. Not that she considered Eddie to be a friend. No matter that the garage was catty-corner to the Museum, she wasn't close enough to call him a friend, not for a long time now. Friendly acquaintance, maybe.

Not that she really had many friends at all. Her best friends didn't live nearby, and neither did most of her acquaintances.

Was she weak to admit this? She didn't see that she had a choice.

Yet, here Eddie was wondering if that body in the bog had been Patricia's. And Effie was fussing about attendance at her Museum. About how no one would notice her. While he'd been so bothered by the Sleeping Woman that he'd had to come see her himself.

"Why didn't you just believe your dad?" she asked.

Eddie snapped his head toward her. "What do you mean?" He looked suddenly defensive, and tired, and old.

No worse than Effie probably looked. When she'd seen herself in the patchy, antique mirror in the bathroom, she had just grimaced and washed her face, hoping for the best. She'd looked like her mother, and at forty-six she didn't think she was old enough to look like her mother. Though people had, all her life, mistaken her for her mother. Which wasn't exactly a compliment.

"Why didn't you believe Eddie after he came over here this morning?"

"Oh, that. I thought you meant, you know, before."

Before. He meant when they were kids. When he was dating Patricia, and they were all graduating from high school, and things went south for him and Eddie IV. Effie hadn't been around for most of that because she'd gone away to college. Far enough away that she couldn't live home, and that had made the break from the local kids she grew up with final. She never did know how to pass back over that bridge.

Eddie looked back down to his shoes.

White sneakers, old man sneakers. With fresh, clean laces. She and Eddie were both old, and getting older at a rate faster than was proportional to the passage of time. They were fossilizing, very slowly. Which, of course, was the typical rate for fossilization. She was definitely getting punchy. It was too much, having this Sleeping Woman here, having to re-examine everything in a new light.

"I guess I just wished there were answers," Eddie finally said. "I didn't want this to be Patricia, but I knew Dad would try to protect me if it was Patricia. I didn't really think he would lie to me, but…"

"But maybe he would," Effie finished.

Eddie nodded. "Maybe. Like he lies to me about what he finds Eddie doing, or whether Eddie came home, or whether he gave Eddie money. Except we both know he's lying even while he's saying those things. He's trying to fix things he can't fix."

Effie just nodded. What could she say to that? She didn't have her mother anymore, didn't have family nearby, didn't have kids. No one to lie to her, or for her, except herself.

She picked at her slacks, trying to smooth the wrinkles from them, at least near the knees. Her suit would have to go to the dry cleaners, which meant a trip to the next town over. Another place no one really knew her.

"It's the hazard of being a mechanic, I guess," he said. "He's not happy unless he's fixing something."

Effie grinned at that. Eddie III was the same as Eddie II. Eddie III was still here trying to fix her after she'd had that little cry earlier.

"I don't think he can fix the Sleeping Woman," she said.

Eddie shook his head. "Nobody's going to fix her now. But I thought, just maybe, he wouldn't tell me if it was Patricia, especially if she looked awful. And then I would hear it from someone who brought their car in to the garage, or at the Diner. I was the last to know when she left, and if this was her, I didn't want to be the last to know now."

How in the world could he have been last to know? Eddie should have been the first to know that Patricia left. But Effie had been away at school then. In a small town like Clarkston, she supposed it was possible Patricia had told someone she was leaving, and then news had spread around town, coming last to Eddie. Or if not dead last, at least not first. Effie had never asked about the breakup. First, it seemed so personal and intrusive, and second, she knew she'd get a lot of commentary with the gossip, and she didn't like the idea of that.

One of the things Effie liked about history was that the associated commentary and gossip were fascinating, yet couldn't hurt the people who experienced the original events anymore. She could sift through details without facing the trauma of a tragedy head-on. And that's all history was: a series of tragedies camouflaged as Important Events. People known by the detritus of their lives as it intersected with the lives of others. Detritus wasn't Effie's favorite word, but it was one she was well-acquainted with. History was just stories of detritus.

*

Effie sat up straight, jostled out of a dream she couldn't remember by the awful feeling that someone was there, right there, looking at her while she slept. But no one was there. She sat alone on the built-in. Her neck ached where she had leaned against the white wainscoting. Had she really fallen asleep? Had Eddie left her there, sleeping? It was rude, wasn't it, to leave her there and not bother to say he was going back home or to the shop? At least he'd left the lights on, instead of sneaking out and leaving her in the dark. She checked her watch: eight o'clock.

A series of thumps from the display room caught her attention. Voices, too, but she couldn't hear what they were saying. She pushed herself to her feet, slipped into her flats, and hurried to the display room door. Should she confront the intruders? Should she sneak around back to her car and call the police? Was someone messing with the Sleeping Woman? Stealing her?

"I got her," she heard, muffled but clear, from inside the room. Eddie's voice. So he hadn't gone home, then.

She pulled the door open and clasped her hand over her mouth.

This room was brightly lit, too. Effie didn't know when was the last time she'd had all the lights on full in here, and she was horrified to see that the woodwork and shelves that she thought of as clean could use a good, solid, going-over. Not dusting, but the sort of chemical-based scrub-down she couldn't do with items on display.

Eddie stood at the foot-end of the display case, with a flat, wheeled dolly under the case. The case itself was unplugged, and the cords to the electronics rested on top. At the head-end of the case, a guy Effie didn't know stood. He had a second dolly under that end, maneuvering it toward the back door.

"Hey, Sleeping Beauty," Eddie nodded to her, following the lead of the guy with his end of the case. "We're just about to load this onto the truck. Ricky, this is Effie Gennings, the Museum director."

The guy stopped moving the case and came over to her, hand out. He was taller than Eddie, taller even than Deena, she thought. Dark hair, dark eyes, and an excited look on his face. He smelled of old sweat, a little skunk-y, and she wrinkled her nose just slightly before she caught herself.

"Ms. Gennings," he said. "I'm glad to meet you."

She shook his hand politely and tried not to show her distaste of the smell. And did not wipe her hand on her slacks, though she considered it.

"I'm Ricky Jeffries," he said. "We emailed?"

"Professor Jeffries," she smiled. At least this wasn't some flunky the University had sent. This was the department head himself. Though he looked much younger in person than in his photo on the University website. Of course, he was in jeans and a University sweatshirt now, not the suit he'd worn for his photo.

"I'm so happy you're willing to sell the display case," Professor Jeffries said. "I stopped at the University and picked up a check just in case you would be willing."

Effie looked at Eddie.

"I told him you're probably willing to consider it," Eddie said.

"I don't know," Effie said. Of course she was willing, but she hadn't thought ahead this far.

"Even if you don't want to sell it, I'd like to transport her in the case," Professor Jeffries said. "I can hook up the controls for the trip. Then put her into a University micro-climate case. But it will take us a few days to get one set up. So at least I hope you will rent us the case. Moving her outside the case could really damage her."

Effie looked at the case. It was the first big display case she'd ever bought, when she and Deena had moved the Museum into this building. Cherry wood finish on the counter-height pedestal, five feet long and a foot and a half wide, glass enclosed, fully climate controlled, and with its own data logger for humidity and temperature monitoring. It was a monster to move, over four hundred pounds, and she wondered if the dollies underneath it could take that weight.

Of course, Professor Jeffries was right. If they took the Sleeping Woman out of that case, it really might damage her. Just getting her in here, the guys from the town had probably done untold damage. Bits of mud and sticks and who knows what else had taken Effie an afternoon to clean from the carpet. She'd tried to save all those bits. They were in a plastic bag inside the storage area of the case, near the electronics. It probably violated all sorts of preservation best practices, but in the end, she'd given up and vacuumed the carpet of the last of the dirt and dust into a new vacuum cleaner bag, then put that bag in plastic and shut it up into the case as well.

She didn't like to think about parts of a dead body remaining here in the museum. Not that people's skin cells sloughing off didn't gross her out, too. But dead parts of a living body was less disturbing than dead parts of a dead body.

Professor Jeffries had pulled out his wallet and now fished out a check.

"The University is willing to pay eight thousand dollars for the case," he said. "When I saw the model you have in the pictures you sent, I was hoping you would sell so we won't have to transfer her to another case at all. She's a beauty of a find."

He looked back at the case with soft eyes and a slight smile.

"You think she's a thousand years old?" Eddie asked.

Jeffries shook his head. "Probably not. The weave on the fabric looks modern to me. But I wouldn't want to say based on just my quick look at her tonight."

"Modern?" Eddie echoed. He looked toward Effie, his eyes large.

"Yeah. Maybe just a few hundred years? That looks a like a loom weave to me. So it would have to be Colonial, earliest," Jeffries said.

"Of course!" Effie stepped forward and looked closer at the Sleeping Woman. She hadn't thought about the blanket the mummy was wrapped in, and she should have. Textiles were her specialty, but the idea of a real dead person in her Museum had blinded her to that fact. That, and that the blanket itself seemed a black, leathery shroud, almost not fabric at all. Some historian she was.

"You can still see some fiber marks on the wrap," she said.

Jeffries nodded. Eddie turned to her and raised his eyebrows.

"The Iroquois Confederacy didn't have woven cloth like that until European settlers came," she explained.

"Right," Jeffries said. He shifted from one foot to the other. "You'll let us at least borrow the case?"

Effie took a deep breath and let it out slowly. "I can sell it," she said. "But eight thousand is a little more than I paid for it."

"Not much more, I bet," Professor Jeffries said, bouncing on the balls of his feet like a kid now. A six-foot-plus kid. "And the University already made the check out. I can't change it."

He held the check out to her, and she took it. She looked down at it and shook her head. Was all this really happening? The check was made out to the Clarkston Museum Fund, which was perfect because it could go into the Museum account directly.

"Thank you so much," Professor Jeffries held out his hand, and she shook it again. She had the distinct feeling she had just given a kid the birthday gift he'd always wanted.

Jeffries turned to Eddie. "Let's get her loaded. My assistant is outside putting the lift down. The hard part will be getting her down those porch stairs. But I have a jack dolly out there. We can use that to support the case down the stairs. I want to keep her level."

*

Effie and Eddie watched Jeffries and his assistant wave as they drove away.

"Thanks for helping them load the case," Effie said.

"Suppose we should have asked him for some identification or something?" Eddie asked.

"I've got a check from the University," Effie said. "That's good enough for me." Besides, she had seen the Professor's picture on the University site, and the truck had the University logo on the doors.

"Are you hungry?"

Effie turned toward him. Even in the dim light on the street, she thought she saw him flush.

"I could eat something. Are you asking me out, Eddie Adams the Third?"

"Gees, Effie, don't use my whole name like

that."

"Almost your whole name."

"Yeah, almost."

"Well?"

"Yeah, Effie, I'm asking you out. But let me take these creepers back to the shop, first." Eddie indicated the two dollies they'd used to move the display case.

"Creepers?"

"That's what they're called. Plus, I want to change my shoes. These are Dad's," he looked down at his white sneakers.

"You're wearing your dad's shoes?" Effie giggled.

"Yeah, I didn't want to track grease over here or anything, so I talked him into switching with me."

"Well, we're all locked up again, so I can just walk with you."

Eddie put a hand up as if to stop her. "No need, you don't want to come over there all dressed nice. You'll brush against something in the garage—"

Effie shook her head. "I'll wait in the store," she said. "Where do you want to eat?"

"Well, unless you want to go for a long drive, there's pizza," he nodded east, toward one end of town. "Or," he nodded west, "there's pizza. The sandwich place is only open for lunch and the Diner is closed for remodeling."

"Pizza it is," Effie laughed. She probably should have known that was the only choice in Clarkston right now.

"Why don't you pull your car over to our lot?" Eddie said. "It's lit better than here."

"Good idea," Effie walked toward her car. "Want a ride?"

"Nope, I'll just carry these back." He leaned down and grabbed each of the creepers by its hand hole and turned, heading toward the garage.

"Be right there," Effie said. She unlocked her Honda and slid in, turned the engine over, and settled back into the seat. She waited for the engine to warm up. She didn't know if it really needed to warm up, but her mother had always impressed on her that a warm engine ran better, needed less maintenance.

Maybe she'd have to get out more, even if it meant sitting alone in the Diner when it re-opened. She didn't even know it was being remodeled, and she knew everything about town history. Or so she thought. Not that remodeling a restaurant was much of an Important Event.

Tomorrow, she'd clean the display room thoroughly. Get all the old dust that was turning to grime off the shelves, while they were still empty.

Eight thousand dollars was a lot of money—she and Deena would have to figure out the best way to spend it. It could cover months of their expenses, even if they bought another, smaller case than the one they'd had. Maybe they didn't need something quite so large.

Or maybe they could upgrade the air handling to the display room and put in quilt racks instead of keeping everything behind glass. Controlling the temperature and humidity of the room directly, putting in special filters to keep out dust and mold— they could keep a lot more items on display, have bigger special events.

Portia's nephew was always nagging Effie for special write ups about his Aunt's quilt collection. Maybe she could invite some of the historians from over by Geneva for a cooperative display. Their quilt collection would complement Portia's perfectly.

"Did you fall asleep again?"

Effie jumped in her seat. Eddie peered at her through the driver's side.

Effie put down her window. "No, I'm wide awake," she said. "Get in, I'll drive."

"But I changed back to my boots," Eddie

said. "They're not that clean."

"Just get in, Eddie," she said, "I have floor mats. And tell me what kind of pizza you like."

CURE FOR THE SLEEPING WOMAN

MORE WORK BY T. M. ADAIR

Contemporary Short Fiction:

Dinner at the Lost Face
   In Sales, you spend some time with clients over dinner. But Winston isn't in Sales. He's the Big Data guy on staff. His new boss insists Winston come along to meet each of their clients over dinner--and the most troublesome account is tonight--but the boss also insists they meet at the Lost Face Restaurant, a decent place but nothing that will impress a cranky client. A short story.

Speculative & Science Fiction:

Plug & I (Offworlder #1)
   Far out on the edge of Strikken-controlled space, a human who calls himself Plug joins the short-term crew of a mining ship. The Deep Sky Company hauler DSC18 is piloted by a slow-rider, a species naturally able to connect into the machine and operate the ship via thought. This slow-rider has led hundreds of humans over his years at the helm. But

what's a pilot do when the genetically modified Plug wants to change things up? A short story.

Plug 2.0 (Offworlder #2)
  Gilberto isn't used to his new implants. He doubts himself, his decisions to throw a stalker off the DSC-18 mining hauler, and his ability to become more than he was originally designed to be. Now, the CEO of Darling Investigations, Inc. has shown up, looking for his grandson, the stalker that Gilberto and Ryde expelled from the ship months ago. A novella.

The Gresmingas Incident (Offworlder #3)
  Gilberto is under increasing pressure to prove himself, both to the clinic back home and to the Company that owns the hauler. But to prove himself threatens both Willa and Ryde. Even if he can find a way to make all three of them happy, what's he to do when his simple demonstration of control over the mining ship goes horribly wrong? A novella.

Gin-Nee's Dance Bar
  Jacqui needs Doc, her brother's med tech and best friend, to explain how it's possible for her brother's memory to be returning. It

shouldn't be possible after re-education. Doc works at Gin-Nee's Dance Bar, and clubbing isn't Jacqui's thing, but her friend Katt comes along. Inside is a scene Jacqui never expected--no wonder Katt was so willing to come when Jacqui called! A sci-fi short story.

Library Friends

Celia loves books and loves the library...and most of the time she loves the friends she makes there, too. Her fondest wish is to take big kid books home to read. But the librarian, Mrs. Immer, doesn't seem to be on Celia's side, and sometimes, neither does Celia's friend Clara. A speculative short story.

Pick Up On Slisker

A story set on the planet Slisker, where pure bred Sliskers, humans, and human-Slisker hybrids co-exist uneasily...Walton chose this pick up from the freelance options the Agency gave him because of the soft target. The human lived in a suburb on the edge of the forest, but without her Slisker mate. No matter his experience, no matter how many agents he'd trained, Walton preferred an easy pick up with little potential for violence. But his target isn't alone, and his pick up takes a surprise turn for the dangerous. A novella.

Poetry by Tracy May Adair:

Stars Crawl Out From Their Caves
   A full-length volume of poetry available in e-book and in paper.

Apples, Figs, Pomegranates
   A chapbook first published in 1993 and now available in e-book only

Blog:

   You can follow Tracy May Adair on her site at adairauthor.com where she blogs about fiction and poetry. Links to publications in on-line journals, poems, and audio clips of the author reading some of her poems can also be found at her site.